Withdrawn

A Very Merry Christmas

by Lauren Cecil
illustrated by Andrew Grey

Grosset & Dunlap
An Imprint of Penguin Group (USA) Inc.

Copyright © 2011 Disney Enterprises, Inc. Based on the "Winnie-the-Pooh" works by A.A. Milne and E.H. Shepard.
All Rights Reserved. Published under license by Grosset & Dunlap, a division of Penguin Young Readers Group,
345 Hudson Street, New York, NY 10014. GROSSET & DUNLAP is a trademark of Penguin Group (USA) Inc. Manufactured in China.

ISBN 978-0-448-45591-4   10 9 8 7 6 5 4 3 2 1

It was Christmas Eve, and Pooh was very excited.
"Only one more day until Christmas!" he said.

Then, suddenly, Pooh remembered something *very* important.

"Oh bother!" he cried. "I forgot to mail the invitations to my Christmas Eve party!"

Pooh trudged through the snow to visit his friend Christopher Robin.

Christopher Robin opened his door, and Pooh said, "I've come to invite you to my holiday party."

"But, Pooh, this says your party is *tonight*!" said Christopher Robin. "Is everything ready?"

"I could use a little help," Pooh admitted.

"Let's start by delivering these invitations!" Christopher Robin replied.

Pooh's friends were very excited to be invited to a holiday party.

And when they heard that Pooh needed help getting ready, they each volunteered.

It wasn't long before everyone was warming up inside Pooh's cozy house.

"First, we should make a list of the things we need," Christopher Robin explained.

Everyone began calling out things: "A Christmas tree!"
"Cookies!" "Decorations!" "Stockings!" "Presents!"
Pooh could hardly write fast enough.

"Why don't we split into groups?" Christopher Robin said. "That way we can get more done!" So everyone divided up and got to work.

Pooh, Christopher Robin, and Piglet found
the perfect Christmas tree.

Kanga, Roo, and Tigger made Christmas cookies.

And Owl, Rabbit, and Eeyore decorated Pooh's house.

Pooh and his friends worked very hard all day.

They finished getting ready for the party just as the sun set.

"Let's start the party!" Pooh said. "Shall we sing some Christmas carols?"

"I'm too tired to sing," Piglet yawned.

"How about a game?" Pooh suggested. "Or some cookies?"

"I believe we wore ourselves out preparing for the party!" Owl explained.

Then Pooh had an idea.

He went into the kitchen and came back with a tray of steaming mugs.

"What's this?" Christopher Robin asked.

"Tea with extra honey and condensed milk," Pooh said. "It always makes me feel better."

"I don't think we'll be needing all those mugs," Christopher Robin whispered.

That's when Pooh looked around. His friends were fast asleep.

"But we didn't even open the presents," said Pooh.
"Silly old Bear," Christopher Robin said. "Spending
time with friends is the best present of all."